Sandy

Chester River Adventist School
305 North Kent Street
Chestertown, MD 21620

Sandy

Lois Eggers, Mary Ellquist, Ruth Wheeler

REVIEW AND HERALD PUBLISHING ASSOCIATION

Washington, DC 20039-0555
Hagerstown, MD 21740

Copyright © 1984 by
Review and Herald Publishing Association

This book was
Edited by Gerald Wheeler
Designed by Richard Steadham
Cover art by Richard Steadham
Type set: 11/12 Corona

PRINTED IN U.S.A.

Review and Herald Cataloging Service

Eggers, Lois
    Sandy, by Lois
Eggers, Mary Ellquist, and Ruth Wheeler.

    1. Decision making. I. Ellquist,
Mary. II. Wheeler, Ruth. III. Title.
        153.8
ISBN 0-8280-0235-5

Contents

Some Bible texts in this book are from the *Good News Bible*—Old Testament: Copyright © American Bible Society 1976; New Testament: Copyright © American Bible Society 1966, 1971, 1976.

Sandy

Parrots

Slumping into her seat, Sandy shoved her math book into her desk. The warm spring sunshine streamed through the open doors of the large classroom, making it bright and pleasant, but she didn't notice. She didn't even see the red tulips blooming in the window boxes.

"Jim is so mean to me," she muttered to herself as she draped her new white sweater over the back of her chair and smoothed the soft, fuzzy yarn. Her brother had teased that morning, "You look like a sheep in that sweater." Then he had run ahead to the car, bleating like a sheep. Sandy sighed. It was hard to be 10 when you had a brother who was 13.

"Hi, Sandy." Carol leaned across the aisle.

"New sweater? Pretty!"

"Oh, hi," Sandy mumbled. She really liked Carol, but right now she didn't feel like talking to her. When Carol turned away, Sandy felt worse than ever. Jim had made her so angry that she had been rude to her best friend.

"Good morning, Sandy," Mrs. Moore, the teacher, stopped by the girl's desk. "Would you like to take this book over to the principal's office for me before school starts?"

"I guess so," she replied without glancing up.

"Is something wrong?" the teacher asked. "You look unhappy."

"Oh, it's nothing." Taking the book, Sandy walked down the hall to the office. She hoped she wouldn't meet Jim. He might say something to make her even more miserable. How she wished Jim wasn't such a tease and that she didn't have such a quick temper.

When Sandy returned, the children were helping the teacher arrange the room. They slid the twenty desks across the carpeted floor and placed them in a wide half circle. A man and woman carried in big birdcages and put them in a circle. A number of parrots sat on the perches in the cages. One great many-colored macaw with a long tail paced back and forth on his perch, and another bird with a bright-red tail muttered to himself.

As soon as the children were seated, Mrs.

Moore told them, "We are going to have a special treat this morning. Mr. and Mrs. Haravey, who own a pet shop in town, are going to tell us how they train birds."

Mrs. Haravey took a parrot from its cage and held it close to her face. The bird leaned against her and rubbed its head lovingly on her cheek.

"Cracker, please. Cracker, please," it begged.

The children laughed, and the bird hid his head against Mrs. Haravey.

"We are especially interested in how you train your birds," Mrs. Moore said. "It must take much time and patience. Where do your birds come from? And how long does it take to train them?"

"Most parrots come from Africa, South America, and Central America. This one is from Panama. Most of my birds were captured in the forest when they were young and then shipped to the United States. Here they are kept in quarantine for forty-five days to make sure they do not have some disease. When I get them the birds are very wild and frightened by the whole experience."

One of the smaller boys named Mike raised his hand. "Aren't you afraid of them with those big bills and sharp claws?"

"Yes, we have to work carefully with them. I begin by being very quiet as I move around the cages. And I always talk to them in a soft voice. When they become a little used to me, I start taming them.

"First I slowly reach into the cage and wrap the bird in a towel. Keeping it wrapped, I hold it in my lap and talk to it. When it is quiet, I begin to stroke its neck feathers. Gradually I pull back the towel and stroke its back. I handle it several times a day until I can remove the towel and the bird will sit quietly in my lap."

"Don't they ever bite you?" Carol questioned. "My grandmother has a parrot and he bites us, hard!"

"I don't like to be bitten, so I'm careful not to give the bird a chance. They'll bite us if they can."

"How do you teach the birds to talk?" Mrs. Moore asked. "That is not a natural thing for a bird to do."

"Parrots in the jungle continually call to each other. I am told that each flock develops a special call that only it uses. That way the birds in a flock stay together. Human conversation is the way our 'flock' of people communicate, and so the parrot begins to accept it as the call of our group."

The children smiled at the idea. "I guess words are our flock call," Jeff, one of the larger boys commented. "The bird learns whatever language it hears, doesn't it? I saw a parrot that could speak Spanish."

"They learn what they hear," Mrs. Haravey

agreed. "We always use the same phrases and words, saying them over and over. This bird can sing several songs, and he can whistle a few tunes. But it takes much repetition to make an impression on its brain. Kindness and patience and repetition are the keys to teaching an animal or bird a new habit."

The Haraveys took other birds from the cages, handling them carefully and gently. Some did little tricks like climbing ladders and swinging from a perch by their beaks.

When the Haraveys had gone, Mrs. Moore said, "Parrots can be lots of fun. My sister and her husband had one when they lived on a ranch in Mexico. Every morning she went out carrying a basket of corn to feed the chickens. When she called, 'Come, chicks! Come, chicks!' they came running and flocked around her while she scattered the corn on the ground. Polly parrot sat on her perch and watched.

"One day while I was visiting my sister we heard the chickens running and cackling. We rushed outside to see what was scaring them. Polly was saying in a voice just like my sister's, 'Come, chicks! Come, chicks!' And the chickens were flocking around the parrot's perch. When she saw the chickens and heard all the cackling, Polly danced on her perch, flapped her wings, and squawked.

"Polly had learned that trick without being taught," the teacher explained. "She had listened to those words every morning until she could repeat them."

"Our neighbor has a cat that rings a bell when he's hungry," Carol said. "She taught him that habit, and now Buddy—that's his name—does it every day."

"Did she tell you how she trained him to do the trick?" Mrs. Moore asked.

"Yes, first she hung a little bell on the cupboard door. She took Buddy's paw and touched the bell with it, then gave him some food he liked. He didn't want to touch the bell at first and tried to pull his paw away. But our neighbor kept working with him several times every day."

"How long did it take before Buddy could ring the bell by himself?" Mike asked.

"I don't think it took much more than a week. But of course she worked with him a lot. She taught her dog, Susie, the same trick at the same time. The cat learned it just as quickly as the dog. But there was a difference. Susie liked to do it, but Buddy didn't. He wanted the food, but didn't care to perform. She could reward the dog just by petting her, but the cat wanted the food."

"Did she teach Buddy anything else?" Mrs. Moore asked.

"Yes, she taught him to roll over, to sit up, shake hands, jump over a yard stick, and play dead.

"Our neighbor said that the cat always

seemed to have a struggle with himself when she asked him to do tricks," Carol went on. "When she wanted him to play dead, he'd walk around the room with his tail straight up and the tip twitching. Then he'd drop down and stretch out.

"The cat didn't like to shake hands, either. When she reached for his paw, he'd look the other way. Then he'd turn back and put out his paw. She said, 'Buddy doesn't want to submit to my will.'"

"It sounds as if he was having a battle in his mind, doesn't it?" Mrs. Moore commented. "He wanted the reward, but he really didn't want to obey."

"I have a new kitten," Sandy said. "Do you think I could teach it some tricks?"

"Yes," Tim replied, "but my dad thinks cats are a lot harder to train than dogs. Dogs will do what they are told just so that you will pet them. But cats seem reluctant to do what they are asked. I don't think cats like to be petted as much as dogs do."

Mike raised his hand. "My dad took me to an animal training farm last summer. They had some tigers and lions that did tricks. A lion came out and jumped up on a high stand and then sat with its front paws in the air. But the trainer had to make it do everything. He had to snap his whip at the lion to make it move, and the lion snarled. It didn't want to obey."

"Thank you for telling us about the animals, Mike. Training an animal is simply teaching it new habits. Tell me, what is a habit?"

"I guess it's doing something the same way over and over until the animal performs it one way every time," Tim, a quiet boy, answered.

"That's true," Mrs. Moore agreed. "Let's imagine that thoughts make impressions or little pathways in the brain. Every time a thought goes through the brain, it wears the pathway a little deeper—like what happens to produce a path on the lawn. It takes a lot of walking, but if people keep it up, a path will appear."

Their teacher picked up a pencil as she spoke, and then she smiled at the children. "I guess you have noticed that holding a pencil is a habit of mine. I think best when I'm holding one."

The children looked at each other. They had all noticed that she always reached for a pencil when she began to talk.

"I want to learn about habits, don't you? I have a friend, Mrs. Hanson, who will be visiting me for two or three weeks. She has made a special study of the mind, and has promised to come to school and talk to you about how the brain works. I thought you would enjoy her talks more if you first saw how the Haraveys trained their birds. She will have worship with us every morning and will explain how we think and choose and learn new habits."

"Do you think she might teach us how to train pets?" Sandy asked. "I'd like to know how to teach tricks to my kitten."

"I think she will. When you learn how your mind works, you may find it fun to try out some new ideas on your pets."

Mainspring

S andy slipped into the classroom just as Mrs. Moore announced, "Boys and girls, I want you to meet my friend, Mrs. Hanson. She is going to be our special guest for a few days."

The girl watched the tall woman walk to the front of the room. Mrs. Hanson's friendly smile reminded Sandy of her grandmother, who could always understand a girl's problems.

"Your teacher has been telling me about your visitors yesterday," Mrs. Hanson said. "I wish I could have seen them. Teaching new habits to animals takes patience and work. But it is fun to do. How the mind works is really a fascinating story, whether the mind belongs to a parrot or to a person.

"I want to talk to you about a most delicate piece of machinery." As she spoke, the visitor walked down the aisle with her watch in her hand, its back open. She stopped at each desk to let the children look at it. "I pried the back off," she explained, "so I could let you see it at work. Notice how the tiny wheels fit together and turn each other. Can you see the mainspring? It's the most important part of the watch."

The children stared at the tiny wheels. Some of the wheels moved faster than others. Tim asked Mrs. Hanson if she wasn't afraid she would damage her watch by taking off the back. What would happen if she dropped it?

"You may be sure I am very careful, but I had to find some way to illustrate what I want to tell you." She laid the open watch on the teacher's desk. "Each of you has a piece of machinery far more valuable than this watch. Can you guess what it is?"

"Is it my heart?" Sandy asked.

"Your heart is important, but I'm not thinking of it just now."

"I know!" Carol said quickly. "It's your brain."

"You're right! Your brain is an important part of you. What can it do that no other part of your body does?"

"Think," Tim suggested.

"Decide," another boy added.

"Remember," chimed in several children.

"Choose what I want to do," Jan, one of the bigger girls stated. "I like to do as I please."

"Think. Decide. Choose. Remember." Mrs. Hanson counted them off on her fingers. "Your brain with all its intricate parts can do all these and much more. It is a most wonderful machine."

At the back of the room Jeff, who was always full of fun, raised his hand. "Do you mean I have wheels in my head?"

"Well, not exactly, but have you ever heard people say they can 'see the wheels turning' when you're thinking hard? Your brain is a large organ of the body. Each area or part of the brain has a special work to do. One part of the brain is for imagination. And right here," Mrs. Hanson touched her forehead, "is the part of the brain that reasons and makes decisions. This is the part that does the thinking."

She took from the desk a drawing of the brain that had the different areas marked on it. The front part of the brain had the label *Thinking*. "This is the most important part of your brain. It is where the will is located." She pointed to the front of the brain. "The will is the part that makes decisions. Here is where you choose what you will do. I like to compare the will to the mainspring in my watch, for it controls other parts of the brain."

As she spoke, Mrs. Hanson wrote on the

chalkboard:

WILL (mainspring) + CHOICE

Then she turned and pointed to a boy sitting across from Sandy. "What choices have you made this morning?"

Sandy wanted to laugh at the surprised look on his face.

"I—I—I guess I chose to ride my bike to school today," he stammered.

Another boy added quickly, "My brother let me choose which ball I wanted to bring to school today."

Several other children volunteered their choices. "I chose cornflakes for breakfast." "I chose to bring my lunch instead of going home at noon." "I chose to bring my jump rope."

"Those are all good decisions. Did any of you make a poor choice this morning? Did any of you choose to be unhappy or angry today? How do you feel this minute? You know, how you feel is your choice too."

Mike raised his hand. "Do you mean if I get mad when somebody trips me, it's my choice? I'm mad before I even have time to think about it."

Sandy looked around quickly to watch his face. She always felt a little sorry for him. His mother was dead, and he lived alone with his father. Sometimes he came to school looking uncared-for. He had a quick temper, and everybody in school knew how many quarrels he had been in.

"Let's think about your problem until tomorrow. Right now I want to talk about your will, the part of your brain that makes choices.

"In the beginning when God created Adam and Eve, He gave them perfect brains. They were free to use their wills to make decisions.

"As soon as God created Adam and Eve, Satan tried to make them choose to disobey God. After a while they listened to the devil. When they chose to disobey God, Satan could control their wills. And ever after that day, he has had power over every person who does not choose to obey God."

Mike burst out without even raising his hand. "Why did God let Satan talk to Adam and Eve? Why didn't He keep Satan away from them?"

The woman smiled. "I can understand your question. It would seem that it would have been best if God had kept Satan away." Mike nodded vigorously.

"Adam and Eve had to be free to disobey God if they chose to. God does not take away a person's free will. Everyone must be free to make his own decisions or choices. But God and His Son rescued Adam and Eve from Satan's control. Then people were free to choose again. Every one of us has the same choice to make that Adam and Eve did. If we let God lead us, we are really choosing the best thing for ourselves."

Carol spoke slowly. "Sometimes I don't know how to choose. And I feel all mixed up inside."

"I understand. Tomorrow we will talk about how to choose," Mrs. Hanson promised.

As the children waited after school for their parents, Sandy turned to Jan and Carol. "What do you think Mrs. Hanson will tell Mike about getting mad? I wonder if she ever had a big brother that teased her."

Carol shrugged. "I don't know. But I wonder if a big brother can be any worse than a little sister who gets into my things all the time. I wish I had my own room and could lock the door."

Jan scowled. "I know how kids are. I've got two brothers. One's older and one's younger, and they make me mad all the time. But they know better than to touch my things. They know what would happen."

"My sister Julie used to get into my things too," Sandy sympathized. "But now she is 8, and she's busy keeping our little brother Danny—he's 2—out of her things. Now it is easier for me to get along with her."

Choice

After the opening exercises at school, Mrs. Hanson turned to Mike. "Can you repeat the question you asked me yesterday?"

"Did you say yesterday that I really choose to get mad when somebody trips me?" the boy asked quickly. "I think it is automatic—something that happens without any of us thinking."

Mrs. Hanson looked at Sandy. "What do you think? Do you believe getting angry is automatic or a matter of choice?"

The girl hesitated. Maybe she would feel foolish if she said what she thought, but Mrs. Hanson's smile encouraged her. "My brother teases me and makes me angry. Do you mean I *choose* to get angry at him? I think it is his fault because he makes me mad."

"Many people believe as you do. They blame another person or thing for the way they feel. Maybe a discussion of anger should be a part of our study of the will and how to make choices. Do you remember what happened to Adam's will?"

Mike leaned forward. "Satan took control of him when he disobeyed God."

"But then Adam and Eve were sorry, and they chose to obey God," Carol added. "And remember, you were going to tell us today how to choose."

Mrs. Hanson nodded in agreement. "Yes, let's talk about choosing. First, you must say to Jesus, 'I choose to obey You.' When you make this choice, you are using your own free will. You are choosing the One who will guide your life."

"When I decide to obey God, is that giving my will to Him?" Tim asked in a solemn voice.

"Yes, by choosing to do right, you are working with God. As soon as you make that choice, God gives you the strength to carry out your plan."

"That doesn't sound too hard," Carol smiled at the woman.

"No, it isn't. Every person is precious to God, and He is waiting to help you." She turned to the rest of the class.

"I said yesterday that the brain can do many different things. A person can think, remember, reason, choose. No one can name all the different activities it can do. Just to help us understand what some parts of the brain do, let's play a little game and pretend that each part is like a little person and that it talks to you. Let's call the parts 'little judges.'

"One part acts as your *conscience.* This little judge or counselor must tell you, 'Yes, it is right,' or 'No, it is wrong.' Did you know that God speaks to each of you through your conscience? He helps you decide what is right and what is wrong.

"Another part of the brain is *reason,* or common sense. It must answer the question 'Is it best? Is it a good idea?'

"Still another part is *desire,* what you want. It says, 'I want it,' or 'I don't want it.'"

Mrs. Hanson turned and wrote on the chalkboard:

> CONSCIENCE: Is it right?
> REASON: Is it best?
> DESIRE: Is it what I want?

"Let's find out how these little judges can help your will make a decision. Now suppose that you meet a friend after school. He says, 'Hey, I want some bubble gum. Let's go by the store on our way home.'

"You answer, 'That's a good idea, but I don't have any money.'

"Your friend replies, 'I don't have any either, but that's no problem. Nobody will catch me.'

"Immediately your conscience, your reason, and your desire start sending messages to your will." She turned to the chalkboard and pointed to the list written there. "What do you think your conscience will say? What question does it ask?"

"I know!" Jeff volunteered. "My conscience would say, 'No, that's not right. Stealing is against the law.'"

"What do you think your reason would reply?"

"I think it would tell me, 'No, that's not best. You might end up in jail,'" Carol replied.

Mrs. Hanson nodded. "Now, what about your desire? What do you really want to do?"

Mike answered, "I think it would still be saying, 'Yes, I want some gum.'"

Mrs. Hanson smiled. "Now, your will must make a decision. Your conscience and your reason say, 'No.' But your desire still declares, 'I want it.'"

"I think my will would say, 'I'm not getting my gum that way,'" Mike continued. "'I'll buy gum when I have some money.'"

"That would be a sensible, conscientious choice," Mrs. Hanson commented. "Your will can tell your desire, 'I will not let you have your way. I choose to listen to my conscience and my reason.' Then your will is in control, and it makes the decision. But you may be unhappy because you are not doing what you really want to do."

Sandy suddenly thought of something, "Sometimes my little brother wants his own way and can't have it, so he screams and cries and even bumps his head on the floor. He has a real temper tantrum."

The children laughed. One of the smaller girls stated, "I can remember when I used to do that."

Mrs. Hanson chuckled. "Yes, I guess we all can remember letting our tempers get the best of us. But when any part of your brain has a 'temper tantrum' and demands its own way, you're in trouble, for a battle is going on in your mind.

"All of you are old enough to make choices," she continued. "But your little judges, the different parts of your brain, must want the same thing if you are to have peace and happiness."

She paused a moment before she finished. "You have to change your thinking until you really want or desire what conscience and reason say is best for you. When conscience, reason, and desire all agree, you can safely listen to desire. This is very important to remember."

The children must have been thinking seriously, for the room was quiet. At last Mrs. Hanson broke the silence. "Do you think you understand how to obey God?" Several children nodded their heads in agreement.

"I think I do," Tim answered. "I ask God to guide my will. Then when I have to make a decision, I ask, 'Is it right? Is it best? What would Jesus have me do?' Then God helps me to choose the right thing to do. Isn't that what you have been telling us?"

"You have stated that nicely, Tim. If we let God guide us, we'll be able to answer those questions correctly."

While Sandy ate her lunch that noon, Jan came and sat beside her. "I don't believe what she says." Her voice showed that she was angry. "I don't have to have something or somebody telling me what to do all the time. I want to be my own boss."

Not knowing how to answer, Sandy didn't say anything. But she was sorry for the other girl. Jan always seemed unhappy. Although she had been at school for a month, she hadn't tried to make friends. Sandy looked at her sitting with her shoulders slumped and her head down. She knew what her father would say if he could see the girl. "Sit up straight, Jan; you are a child of God and you're important to Him." But she knew that it wouldn't do for her to make this suggestion— not now, anyway.

"Old Junky"

The children had crowded around Mr. and Mrs. Knight at the front of the room when Sandy arrived at school. The Knights were an elderly couple who lived just down the street. The children had adopted them as their class 'grandparents.'

This morning the Knights had brought a big old clock and set it on the end of a table. They had placed it with its open back toward the children so that the class could see its wheels turning. The clock's long pendulum hung almost to the floor.

When the children had found their seats, the woman told the clock's story. "One of our friends who knew that Mr. Knight liked to fix antique clocks brought us several tin cans full of wheels, springs, and other parts of an old clock. It looked like a lot of junk. My husband worked many days sorting, polishing, and putting the parts together. When he was through, the old clock ran and kept good time. He called it 'Old Junky.' He wants you to keep it here in your schoolroom for a few days so that you can watch it work."

Before they left, Mr. Knight pointed out a place on the wall where he thought the old clock should hang. "Right here in the front of the room, high on the wall, would be a good place. All of you can see it here."

The children all enjoyed watching the wheels of the clock turn, and Mrs. Moore decided to leave it on the table where they could see it. Since Mr. Knight said it must be level, she carefully propped it up. She unhooked the pendulum and laid it on the table because it hung down in the way, and the children might stumble over it and knock the clock off the table.

When Mrs. Hanson came at nine-thirty, she was delighted to see the beautiful old clock. But by then something had gone wrong. The clock was running much too fast. Even as they watched, it struck twelve-thirty.

"Something is wrong," Mike commented. "It's going too fast. It's striking another hour every fifteen minutes."

"I've been keeping track," another boy said, "and it's gained four hours since Mr.

Knight set it for eight-thirty. What do you think is wrong?"

"It acts as if it's on drugs, doesn't it?" Mrs. Hanson observed.

"On drugs!" The children looked at her puzzled. "How could a clock be on drugs?"

"That's what some drugs do to you," Mrs. Hanson insisted. "They speed up your brain until it doesn't work right. Your brain sort of burns itself out because its thought patterns become all mixed up." She turned to the clock. "I'm glad we have this fine old clock to observe for a few days." She leaned down and studied it more closely. "Where is the pendulum?"

"Here it is." A boy pointed to a long thin strip of wood lying on the table. At the end of the wood was a shiny piece of metal as big as a saucer.

Mrs. Hanson picked up the pendulum and examined it for a few moments, then glanced at the clock. "Boys and girls, I think I know the secret of why Old Junky is running too fast. You all know what rules and laws are. Can you tell me some of the laws that you obeyed on your way to school today?"

The children talked about stop signs, about walking on the left side of the road, about facing traffic if there isn't a sidewalk. Someone suggested that no one should cross the street in the middle of the block.

"There is a reason for each of the laws you

have mentioned," Mrs. Hanson commented. "They all help you walk in a way that is safe. But what does this have to do with the clock? What might be the reason it is not doing what it is supposed to do?"

"Is Old Junky where Mr. Knight told you to put it?"

"No," Jeff explained. "He told us to hang it on the wall, but we wanted it on the table where we could watch the wheels turn."

"And we took the pendulum off too," Carol added.

"You've told me what you did do with the clock, but let's think about what you didn't do."

Tim leaned forward. "You mean all we have to do is hang it on the wall, put the pendulum back on, and it will keep the right time?"

"Let's try it," Mrs. Hanson suggested. The children helped mount the clock on the wall. They attached the pendulum to the little hook at the back of the clock. Then Mrs. Hanson started it swinging. The clock ran for a few seconds, but it stopped.

"Maybe it needs winding," Mike suggested.

"Let's try that." Mrs. Hanson reached up and found the key in the back of the clock and carefully wound it. Once more she swung the pendulum, and this time it kept on swinging.

"What is the pendulum for?" one of the

children asked.

"Watch and listen carefully." Mrs. Hanson unhooked the pendulum. At once the clock ticked much too fast. Then she replaced the pendulum and the clock again ticked slowly and evenly.

"I know!" Mike nearly jumped out of his seat. "The pendulum is heavy and it slows the clock down. Without the pendulum to hold it back, it runs four times too fast."

"You've discovered the secret, Mike. This beautiful old clock was built to run with a pendulum just this length and weight. That is the principle on which it works. The clockmaker knew exactly how heavy and long to make the pendulum for this size clock."

"A small clock would need a short pendulum, and a big one a long, heavy one," Jeff decided.

"That's correct. Each size of clock must have a pendulum of just the right length and weight. That's a rule the clockmakers must know."

She turned and looked at the tall old clock ticking away. "The clockmaker must have taken great pride in making this wonderful machine. He must have made the very best clock he could. And after maybe a hundred years it is still a good clock, keeping good time."

Carol raised her hand. "I think the clockmaker would be happy to know how Mr.

Knight has cleaned and shined all the parts and made the clock beautiful again."

Mrs. Hanson stepped closer to the children. "I am sure he would be. You know, I'd like to compare this clock to a human being. God, the Creator, made the very best persons He could. He created a perfect man and a perfect woman. In fact, He made them something like Himself, and He gave each a brain that was able to reason. Just as the wheels and springs in the clock must work together, so our brain has many parts that must function smoothly together. Tell me, what is one of the things your brain does?"

"Think!" Jeff burst out.

"You're right, Jeff. That's one part of its role, but it has many, many other things it can do. Our Master knows how your brain works best. He has set rules for its use. You remember that the clockmaker had to figure out just how to keep the clock working best. What were some of the rules Mr. Knight gave?"

"Hang the clock on the wall," someone suggested.

"Put the right size pendulum on it," another child added.

"We have an old clock," Tim said, "and my dad winds it every week. He oils and cleans it, and it keeps good time."

Mrs. Hanson nodded. "All those are important for clocks. Do you think there are things you need to do to keep your brain working well? When do you think best?"

"When I'm not sleepy," Sandy said.

"And when I'm not hungry," Jeff added.

"I think fastest when I'm running out-of-doors and my brain is getting lots of oxygen," Tim suggested.

"And don't use drugs," Mike said. "They keep your brain from working right."

"You've named four important ways to keep your brain working well." Mrs. Hanson counted them off on her fingers. "Plenty of sleep. Good food; no junk foods. Exercise out-of-doors. No drugs. There are more ways to take good care of the brain, but these four are important. When you obey your Maker's rules, you are protecting the finest computer ever made—your brain."

Wrong Thinking

Mrs. Hanson glanced around the room as she stood beside the desk for her morning worship talk. "It sounds by all the chatter I heard as I came in that you have a lot to tell me. Let's turn to Proverbs 23:7 and read it together for our thought for the day. It will tell you what a man really is."

The children took their Bibles from their desks and quickly found the verse. They read, "As he thinketh in his heart, so is he."

"Does anyone have another version of the Bible?" Mrs. Hanson asked.

One of the boys raised his hand. "I have a *Good News Bible*. I'll read the verse from that. 'What he thinks is what he really is.'"

"Thank you," Mrs. Hanson said. "Because

thinking is so important, I want to talk with you about your mind and what you think." She opened a big flat box she had laid on the teacher's desk when she came in. From it she lifted a large framed motto and showed it to the children. Bright flowers bordered a hand-lettered motto. Mrs. Hanson read the words:

"'Plant a thought, reap a feeling.
Plant a feeling, reap an act.
Plant an act, reap a habit.
Plant a habit, reap a character.
Plant a character, reap a destiny.'"

"Your destiny is what happens to you. You and I want to spend eternity in heaven with God. That is the destiny we hope for. But our destiny begins with our thoughts. And, as you see, our thoughts are followed by feelings, acts, and habits. And all together," she pointed to the motto, "they form the character. We are going to talk about these first two today: thoughts and feelings."

Mike raised his hand. "I've tried all week not to get upset about things, but still I'm mad sometimes. What can I do about my feelings?"

"I've been hoping we could talk about this, Mike."

"Sandy waved her hand. "I'd like to know what to do about my feelings too."

"Me, too!" chorused several other voices.

"Here's how it works. In a way it's like math." Mrs. Hanson turned to the board and wrote as she spoke. "Thinking produces feelings. And thinking plus feelings equals actions. Let's write it this way:"

Thinking $\longrightarrow$ Feelings

Thinking + Feelings = Actions

"Now I'm going to write it another way, and you tell me how it should be."

Bad thoughts $\longrightarrow$ Bad feelings

That was as far as she got before the children exclaimed,

"Bad thoughts produce bad feelings.

Bad thoughts plus bad feelings equals bad actions."

Mrs. Hanson clapped her hands. "That is exactly the way it is! Now let's turn it around." Quickly she erased the word *bad* and replaced it with *good*. The children repeated as she printed:

"Good thoughts produce good feelings.

Good thoughts plus good feelings equals good actions."

Laying down her chalk, she said, "Once you know the rule, or principle, you can stop trying to change your actions. The actions aren't the beginning of the problem. Where does each start?"

"With thinking," the children responded.

"Right! You've made an important discovery. Let's put it another way:"

Changed thoughts + changed feelings = changed actions

"But how can I control what I think?" Jeff

demanded. "Seems to me that my head is just a jumble of thoughts."

With a smile Mrs. Hanson agreed. "Yes, our thoughts do seem to whirl around like falling leaves on a windy day. But you can learn to control what you think. That is part of growing up. If you really want to accomplish something, you must learn to think straight while you are young."

"Pardon me for interrupting," Mrs. Moore said from where she sat in the back of the room, "but I just heard something last night I want to share with you. Twin boys were born in a cabin in the hills of North Carolina. They were identical twins. Even their parents couldn't tell them apart. When their mother died, the father gave a boy to each of the grandmothers.

"One grandmother sent her child all the way through school. The other grandmother lived out in the mountains where there was only one small school. She didn't care if the boy went to it or not, so he roamed the hills and fished.

"Somebody who was studying twins got the boys together when they were men. They still looked alike. However, the man who had grown up in the mountains didn't care about working or doing anything worthwhile, but his brother had gone to college and become a teacher."

"Thank you," Mrs. Hanson said. "That's a

good illustration. An education does develop the power to think and to do. Your brain is a wonderful machine. You should develop it as much as you can.

"Let's come back to Mike's question about his thoughts. There is something we can do to change the way we think and feel." She paused a moment before she continued. "I'm going to tell you a very personal experience. I used to be a crybaby. If I was afraid or angry, I would cry. Even when I was grown and the mother of several children, I still cried. I couldn't control my tears, and I often embarrassed myself. What was I to do?

"My friends suggested that I cried because I was feeling sorry for myself. Although I was sure that I was not doing it for that reason, I finally agreed to think about it. After a while I thought my way back to childhood. When I was a little girl, I often saw my father whip my brothers and sisters. Naturally I was afraid of him. And soon I learned that if I cried, he wouldn't punish me. My tears saved me every time.

"When I was a teenager I had to miss one day of school a week to help with the washing and ironing. It wasn't fair, and I had good reason to feel sorry for myself. To make matters worse, my brothers wouldn't help me. I cried because I was tired and angry.

"As I thought back over my childhood, I realized that I had good reason to cry then.

But now I was grown and had my own home, conditions were different, and I didn't need to cry anymore.

"For two years I tried to stop feeling sorry for myself, but I still couldn't control my tears. Finally I studied God's Word and realized what the problem was. I had been working on my feelings when I should have been changing my thinking. I had to find out what my wrong thinking was before I could replace it with right thinking."

Again she paused and smiled at the children. "Can you figure out, from what I've told you, what my wrong thinking was?"

"Was it that you were afraid?" Mike asked. "Were you still afraid of your father?"

"That's part of it," the woman agreed. "What else might I have been thinking that was wrong?"

"Maybe you thought you were a slave," Carol suggested.

"You're right. I did. I thought I was inferior to other people. Where had my thinking gone wrong?"

Too puzzled by what Mrs. Hanson was telling them, the children didn't answer.

"I was thinking that other people were better than I was," she continued, "and that I should always take second place. And that made me feel sorry for myself. I had to admit that my friends were right. My problem was self-pity. When I began to think that I was a person loved by God and that I could do what other people could, I no longer had a reason to be sorry for myself. I knew that God would help me be a worthwhile person. And you know, my tears stopped!"

The children shifted in their seats. Sandy was glad she had heard the woman's story. She looked up at the speaker's happy face. No one would ever imagine that she had been once a crybaby and had felt sorry for herself. Then Sandy thought of her own feelings.

"Sandy, you look like you are thinking hard. Would you like to tell us about it?" The woman's smile was so warm and encouraging that the girl felt she could share what was going through her own mind.

"I just realized that when my brother teases me and I get angry, my angry feelings come from what I think. Then I come to school feeling angry and don't want to talk to Carol. I ignore her and won't answer when she speaks to me."

Walking down the aisle, Mrs. Hanson put her hand on Sandy's shoulder. "You're right in concluding that your angry feelings come from your angry thoughts." She turned to the other children. "What do you think Sandy could do about her brother's teasing?"

"She could slap him down," Jan snapped. "Brothers are mean."

Sandy saw that Jan's face was flushed and angry.

"Yes." Mrs. Hanson's voice was gentle. "That's one thing she could do. But would that help anybody? It might make matters worse."

Jeff turned to Sandy. "Maybe if you didn't get mad, Jim wouldn't think it was fun to tease you. Maybe you could try not getting mad and see what happens."

After a moment's thought, Sandy nodded her head in agreement.

When she reached home that afternoon she quickly changed her clothes and went into the kitchen to help. Mother handed her a stack of clean towels. "Please take these upstairs and put them away."

Just as Sandy turned to start up the stairs, Jim popped out of the dining room on his way upstairs with his flash camera. Sandy caught her toe on a small rug, and the next thing she knew, she was on the floor with towels scattered all around her.

Her brother laughed. "You should see yourself! I've got to have a picture of this." He snapped the camera and ran up the stairs.

Furious, Sandy knew how silly she looked, all sprawled out with towels everywhere. "There he goes, making fun of me," she muttered. "And he'll have a perfectly ridiculous picture of me to show."

Picking herself up, she began to stack the towels. The more she thought about Jim and his camera, the more angry she became. I'll get even with him, she promised herself. I'll smash his old camera.

Then partway up the stairs she caught herself. "That's not right!" she said to herself. With every step she took, the thought repeated itself, Not right! Not right! That must be my conscience, she thought. Do unto others as you would have them do unto you. Yes, that was conscience.

Another thought flashed into her mind. Cameras cost money. It would be throwing away money to break one. Now reason was talking to her, she realized. But she still felt that she should punish Jim somehow, because he was always making fun of her. "I'll just teach him a lesson," she sputtered. Then Jan's angry face flashed into her mind. That was the way Jan would handle the problem, Sandy was certain.

Slowly Sandy went up the stairs, her mind in a whirl. Conscience, reason, and desire all seemed to be talking at once. She stopped at the head of the stairs and thought, then went to stack the towels in the linen closet. Finally she said half out loud, "I won't do it. Jesus will help me not to retaliate against Jim."

As she turned to go down the stairs, she saw her brother standing in the doorway of his room. She smiled at him, and he had the most puzzled look on his face.

"I hope you let me see that picture before you take it to school," she said as she started down the stairs. To her surprise, she really didn't feel angry any more.

Humming to herself, she began setting the table. "You sound happy," her mother said. "I thought you would be mad at your brother for taking your picture."

"I was. I wanted to break his camera."

"What changed your feelings?"

"I thought about what Jan said and how she looked." Her words tumbled out as she told her mother about the girl and the things she had been saying at school. "She looks so angry most of the time, and she doesn't have any friends, either. I feel sorry for her. I try to be nice to her, but she doesn't seem to notice."

Mother stirred the soup for a moment. "Jan probably doesn't like herself very well. Wouldn't you like to invite her to go skating with you and Carol? I'm sure she really needs friends."

"I'll call Carol tonight and ask her. Maybe we can change the way Jan feels and thinks. I hope so."

Instincts

After dinner Sandy's father suggested that the family go for a walk. "I found a killdeer's nest in the meadow and would like to see if you can find it too."

Father set little Danny on his shoulders and led the way as they followed an old gravel road. Julie ran ahead. "What does a killdeer's nest look like?"

Before her father could answer, Sandy said, "The killdeer doesn't make a nest. She just lays her eggs on the ground. The eggs look like gravel and are hard to find."

"That's right." Father looked carefully about his feet. "The eggs are right along here somewhere, in the middle of the road."

Jim leaned over and picked up a round

white pebble speckled with black. "Don't the eggs look like this?"

"Yes, they are about that size and color. I was sure they were along here somewhere."

"I think I know what happened," Jim said. "Look at the killdeer over there by the grass. She keeps walking along and watching us. I think she has her babies over there."

Father glanced up. "I think you're right. Let's follow her and see what she does."

The family left the road and headed toward the killdeer. The bird ran into the plowed field, dragging a wing as though she were badly hurt.

"You're right, Jim," Father said. "She is trying to lead us away. Let's look by the grass where we first saw her. She may have left them there."

Suddenly right at her feet Sandy saw a baby killdeer huddled on the ground. "I've found a baby," she called as she reached down and picked up the little bird. It lay limp in her hand.

"Daddy, look at him. Is there something the matter with him? Maybe I've scared him to death."

"Isn't he cute," Julie said, "Can I hold him?" And Danny held out his hands too.

"I think he's all right." Father looked at the bird. "But I don't think we ought to frighten him more. Let's put him down and see what he does."

Sandy laid the limp little bird on the ground and stepped back. Jim paused by the bird for a moment. Then just as he started to leave, the mother bird, who had been watching, gave a sharp call. The fledgling jumped up and began to run. As it raced past Jim, he reached down and picked it up. But the little bird wriggled right between his fingers and sped toward its mother.

"Look at him go!" Jim laughed. "The little rascal! How could he be weak and then suddenly be strong enough to run like that?"

As the family watched they saw another baby, and then still another, run toward the mother bird. "There are four babies!" Jim exclaimed.

"What made him lie so still while I had him?" Sandy asked. "I thought he was dying."

"We call that *instinct*," her father explained. "These baby birds have to know how to obey their mother's calls just as soon as they are hatched. When the mother saw us coming, she gave a call that meant 'Sit still,' and those babies obeyed."

"But he couldn't stand up. He was as limp as if he were dead," Sandy insisted.

"You're right, Sandy. His instinct was so strong that he had to obey it. He couldn't run or even stand up."

"But when I had him he was so strong that I was afraid to hold him tight enough to hang on to him," Jim added.

"That was instinct too. His mother told him to run and he had to run. It wasn't anything he chose to do," Mother explained.

"Don't you wish I obeyed like that?" Julie looked up at her mother's face.

"No. I want you to obey because you think about it and choose to obey. Wild birds and animals don't choose. They cannot go against their instincts unless someone trains them to do so."

As they crossed the meadow, Sandy asked, "Don't people have any instincts?"

"Yes, Sandy," Father answered. "They have some. Do you remember how tightly Danny held on to your finger when he was tiny? Holding on and fear of falling are two instincts of a human baby. But humans have brains that God created to reason. People are free to decide and to make choices. They have common sense and can figure things out for themselves. Thus they can choose to obey God even when it goes against their natural instincts."

Sandy picked up a pebble and tossed it. "Yes, I know. We've been learning that at school. But I wish I didn't have to decide so many things for myself. I'd like to obey without thinking or choosing."

Father laughed. "But then you wouldn't be a person, Sandy. People are made in the image of God. He created them to be His children, and He wants them to reason and make decisions and choices."

"It isn't so difficult, Sandy," Mother said. "God not only gives us minds to reason; He also helps us to make right decisions."

That evening as they sat on the front porch and watched the sunset, Father read the text "Thou wilt keep him in perfect peace, whose mind is stayed on thee" (Isaiah 26:3). "God is telling us not to worry, for He will guide our thinking," he explained. "The instinct that animals have for obedience helps to keep them safe. A bird is hatched knowing how to build its nest and which foods to eat. It knows how to feed and care for its young."

"And bird babies are with their parents such a short time," Mother interrupted, "that the parents couldn't possibly teach them all the things they must know to survive. Even though Danny is 2 years old and is learning many things, he couldn't care for himself, not even for one day. But 2-year-old killdeer have families of their own."

After a moment of silence, Sandy said, "People babies stay with their parents a long time, don't they?"

"Yes," Mother answered. "Human babies have so much more to learn. They have to discover how to make right choices and to tell the difference between what is right and what is wrong. That is why God gives us our children for so many years. I'm glad He planned it that way."

Julie leaned against her mother. "I'm glad I'm not a baby killdeer."

Father ruffled her hair. "We are, too, little sister. We need you. We all need each other, and we all learn from each other. I thank God for my family, every one of you."

After Sandy went to bed she lay awake and stared out the window at the bright stars. Far away an owl hooted, and another answered. She thought about the killdeer babies cuddled under their mother's feathers. Suddenly she had such a warm, happy feeling as she realized she was part of a family, and they loved her. And all the wild creatures and all the people were a part of God's family. He watched over them all.

Changing Habits

As soon as Mrs. Moore had finished the opening exercises she said, "We've been talking about the brain for several days. Do you have any questions you'd like to ask Mrs. Hanson?"

Sandy was the first to raise her hand. "How do you change a bad habit? Jerry, our neighbor boy, is in the first grade, and he still sucks his thumb, even at school. He wants to stop, and all the children are trying to help him, but he still does it. Is there anything I could do to help him? He likes me and plays at our house a lot."

"Yes, there is," Mrs. Hanson began. "Let's talk today about the principles of breaking a bad habit." She pointed to the framed motto that the class had hung on the wall in the front of the room. "The main words on the motto are—" And the children repeated as she pointed:

"Thought. Feeling. Act. Habit. Character. Destiny."

"Where does it all start?" she questioned.

"With thoughts."

"That's right. Let's figure out what is going through Jerry's mind when he sucks his thumb. Then maybe we can figure out new thoughts for him. New thoughts will bring new feelings, and new thoughts and new feelings will bring—?"

"New actions," the children all chorused.

"Like no thumb-sucking? What might Jerry be thinking when he sucks his thumb?"

The boy in front of Carol raised his hand. "He might think, I'm hungry."

Another boy suggested, "Maybe he's sleepy."

"He's thinking, I'm bored," Jan put in. "It's easy to get bored when there's nothing to do."

"Probably you are all correct," Mrs. Hanson observed. "What new thoughts can you suggest for Jerry?"

"If he's hungry, he could get a drink. That helps," someone answered.

"When I'm bored, I look for something else to do," Jan explained.

"He could do all of those things. All three of you are suggesting, though, that Jerry knows what he's doing. Admitting that he is a thumb-sucker is the first step in his breaking the bad habit. Jerry must say to himself, 'Look here, you're sucking your thumb again. Why are you doing that? You don't want to be a thumb-sucker, do you?' Once he thinks like this, his feelings will change. And he'll stop sucking his thumb. Grown people have to struggle to change habit patterns too.

"Did you know that Ellen White tells about the steps she took in changing her eating habits?"

When Mrs. Hanson sat down at the desk in the front of the room, the children knew she was ready to tell them a story. "God told Ellen White about the best foods for good health. She saw that meat was not the best type of thing to eat. Also she realized that whole-grain bread would be better for her than white bread.

"Mrs. White, as she related her experience, said she often ate meat. When she didn't have it, she felt weak and faint. But when God showed her a better diet, she stopped eating meat and white bread. Beginning to feel faint, she would fold her arms over her stomach and announce to herself, 'I will not eat a morsel. I will eat what God told me to eat or I will not eat at all.'

"Mrs. White said that bread was especially distasteful to her, especially whole-grain bread. When she changed her eating habits, she had a special battle to fight.

"Can you imagine, boys and girls," Mrs. Hanson went on, "that God's messenger would have such a terrible struggle with her habits?"

"I guess she really had trouble," Mike commented.

With a nod, Mrs. Hanson continued. "Mrs. White wrote, 'The first two or three meals, I could not eat. I said to my stomach, "You may wait until you can eat bread." In a little while I could eat bread, and graham bread, too. This I could not eat before; but now it tastes good, and I have had no loss of appetite.'"

Mrs. Hanson looked around the room. "Isn't that an amazing story? It's hard to believe, but it's true."

Sandy glanced at the picture of Ellen White on the wall. "I never thought God's messenger would have to struggle to do right. I had always assumed that everything good just came naturally to her."

Mrs. Hanson smiled. "God's messenger wrote, and we may read it, that a person may entirely change his life through the right use of his power of choice. And God helps us make those right choices. He helps us to change our actions. Do you remember the steps I followed in breaking my habit of crying?"

Carol raised her hand. "First, your friends told you that you were feeling sorry for yourself, and you agreed to think about it."

"And after thinking about it, you decided they were right," Jeff added.

"Since my feelings began with my thinking, I had to start changing my thoughts," Mrs. Hanson said. "It helps to change our thoughts if we identify our feelings. We can call them by name if we want. For example, we can say, 'I am shy.' 'I am jealous.' 'I am lonely.'" She paused a moment. "What was my next step?"

"Didn't you think back to the time when you first learned that tears kept you from being punished?" Carol asked.

Mrs. Hanson agreed. "Yes, I had to trace the feeling back to its beginning, and to recall the experiences and thoughts that started the feeling. Do you remember what caused me to cry so easily?"

"You thought you were a slave to your family," Mike answered. "But when you weren't at home and didn't have to work for your family, you had no reason to feel sorry for yourself anymore."

"Right, Mike. Then I asked myself if conditions had changed since then, and if I still needed to feel the same. And once I realized where my thinking was wrong, I could replace those incorrect thoughts with new ones."

Mrs. Hanson paused a moment before she added, "The good, good news for all of us is that our feelings and actions will correct themselves when the thoughts are right. And the best news of all is that God's power is always there to help us choose to think and do the right things.

"You see, as soon as our thinking is right, we begin to have good feelings. Our old feelings that were harming us change into good ones, and this transforms our whole lives."

Plant an Act

Mrs. Hanson reached into her purse and brought out her key ring. She held it up so that the children could see. Sandy smiled when she noticed that a long brown cord attached the ring of keys to the woman's purse.

"This is my habit-forming cord. I was always losing my keys. When I came to the checkout counter in the store, I sometimes laid them on the counter and then went off and forgot them. I've left them in the lock of my post office box. Once I even locked the car door with my keys still inside. And that was awful." She shook her head and looked so sad that the children laughed.

"How do you think this is going to teach me a habit?" She held up the keys on the cord.

"What does our motto say about 'plant a habit'?

Jeff pointed to the motto.

"Plant a thought, reap a feeling.
Plant a feeling, reap an act.
Plant an act, reap a habit."

"Thànk you, Jeff. What is the habit I want to learn? How will this brown cord help me?"

Sandy had an idea. "I think you are trying to learn to put your keys in your purse every time you are through using them," she said. "When you have the habit, you won't even need to try to remember. You will just drop your keys into your purse every time."

The woman's smile broadened. "That is exactly what I am working toward, but how does the cord help me?"

"Because now you *have* to put them back in your purse or they will be dangling," Mike laughed. "You force yourself to think about what you are doing."

Mrs. Hanson laid the keys on the desk. "When the cord makes me think, an electric impulse or a little current goes from my brain to my hand. It says, 'Put keys in purse,' and I obey. Remember how each impulse strengthens the impression?"

"Like wearing a path on the lawn," Jeff interrupted.

"Yes, when the habit becomes strong enough, the impulse will run to my hand without my brain giving the order. When I have the habit formed, I'll drop the keys into my purse every time. In fact, I may not even remember afterward that I did it. But my keys will always be where they belong."

Next Mrs. Hanson picked up a piece of chalk. "Let's make a list of some habits you might like to have, and then we can decide what you could do to develop them."

As the children named habits, she wrote them on the chalkboard:

Hang up my coat as soon as I take it off.

Put my schoolbooks on my desk at home so I can find them quickly in the morning.

Not open the refrigerator door as soon as I get home.

Not eat between meals.

Pray before I go to sleep at night.

Work fast and not fool around.

Always be on time.

Keep my room neat and clean.

"That is a very good list." She turned to the children. "Let's work on the first habit you suggested. 'Hang up your coat as soon as you take it off.' What do you suppose you could do to start that habit? Think about the cat and dog who learned to ring a bell. What did their owner do to get them started?"

Carol raised her hand. "She gave them a reward of food. Could I give myself a reward every time I hang up my coat? But what kind works best?"

"You're really getting the idea. What do some of the rest of you think?"

"I guess she could use anything she liked as a reward," Sandy suggested.

"I could put a penny or a nickel into a jar every time I hung up my coat," Carol said. "Then I could use that money to get something I wanted very much."

"Maybe your parents would give you a reward," Mike suggested. "I think my dad would give me something to get me to hang up my coat. He's always saying that I don't take care of my things."

"How about giving yourself points on the calendar?" another boy offered. "At the end of the week you could count the points and get a reward, like going skating."

"Those are all good ideas," Mrs. Hanson commented. "But what could you do if none of these things worked and you kept on forgetting to hang up your coat? What other ways could you try?"

"I think I need someone to remind me," Sandy said. "Maybe a friend who is working on the same habit could check up on me every other day to see how I am coming. It's more fun to do things together. We could call each other after school and see how the other one is doing."

"I like that suggestion, Sandy," Mrs. Hanson told her. "We all need some kind of support when we are trying to start a new habit."

"Wouldn't it help if I have a special place where I always hang my coat?" a class member asked. "I could practice hanging up my coat in this special place as soon as I took it off, instead of throwing it on a chair, as I usually do."

"Having a system or plan helps," Mrs. Hanson agreed. "Then you do the act in the same way each time, and that is important when you are developing a new habit." She paused and studied their faces a moment, as if deciding how best she should say something.

"How you see yourself makes a big difference when you are changing your habit patterns," she said after a moment. "You must begin to think of yourself as the kind of person who hangs up his coat. Try telling yourself, 'I've grown up enough to care for my things and my room.' Then you will discover that you really do feel grown-up and responsible."

Sandy sat up straight in her seat. "My mother says I am old enough to care for my own room. And I do try to clean my room before I leave for school. Then when I come home, I can go to a neat room and feel happy with myself."

Carol added, "But lots of times I get busy doing something else and I don't have time.

And my mother leaves my room just the way it is. When I come home and walk into that messy room, I don't like myself. I feel unhappy with everybody in the family, and it is all my own fault."

Mike raised his hand. "My dad goes to work early, and I'm supposed to clean up my room and the kitchen, too. But lots of times I don't get it done. Then when Dad comes home, he's cross with me, and I'm mad too. And everything goes wrong. How can I make myself get things done? Lots of times I do clean things up, though, and then when Dad gets home, he's happy and I feel really good."

"Getting control of yourself and making yourself do what you should is part of growing up, Mike. Just keep the picture in your mind of how good you feel when you have cleaned things up. You know, it usually doesn't take long to do the work you are supposed to do. It's mostly a matter of getting right at it and not doing something else first. A good motto is 'Put first things first.' "

With a grin Mike answered, "I know, but sometimes I stop and look at television. Then I have to run to catch the school bus, and naturally I leave the house a mess."

Mrs. Hanson turned to Sandy. "Did you have a chance to work on the thumb-sucking problem with your little friend Jerry? Did you try out some of our suggestions?"

"Yes, I did. I asked his mother for a baby

picture of Jerry that showed him sucking his thumb. Showing it to him, I said, 'Thumb-sucking is a baby habit. Don't you think you should stop now that you are a big boy going to school?'

"He looked at the picture, frowned, then said, 'I'm no baby. I'm going to stop that.' I told him that he must think of himself as a big person who doesn't suck his thumb, and he must keep reminding himself that he is a big boy."

Nodding in approval, Mrs. Hanson said, "You are using the right method, Sandy. Keep talking with him, and let us know what happens." She looked around the room. "It is fun to form new habits. As you think more and more about your brain and how God expects you to use it, you will be making new thought habits. Then your feelings and your actions will change before you realize it. Remember, God has promised to help you."

Picking up her purse, she turned to go, only to have her keys dangle at the end of the long brown cord. She laughed when Mike shouted, "Your keys!"

"I'm really having a struggle," she told him, "but someday I'll have a new habit."

Jan

Sandy and Carol walked together out to the playground at recess. "What do you think of Jan?" Sandy asked. "What makes her act mad at everybody all the time?"

"I don't know, but she's no fun to be with." Carol glanced across the playground at Jan, who stood by herself, watching the younger children play. Thin and taller than the other girls in her grade, she stood with her shoulders slumped.

"She never acts like she wants to talk to us. And when she does say something, it's just to gripe about the school and the town."

Sandy watched the children running and playing. "My mother says that maybe Jan doesn't like herself, and that's why she thinks people don't like her. I'd like to be friends with her, if I knew how. It's no fun standing around watching other people play and always thinking they don't want you around. I feel sorry for her."

"You can try to be friends if you want to," Carol answered, "but don't be surprised if she snaps your head off."

Taking her friend's arm, Sandy said, "Let's try together. If I invite Jan to go skating tomorrow after school, you'll go with us, won't you? Maybe we can get her to tell us what is making her mad all the time."

After a hesitation Carol replied slowly, "Yes, I'll go, but you're the one that is going to ask her, not me."

With that much of a promise, Sandy skipped to the other side of the playground and stopped by Jan. But the girl ignored her. Jan doesn't know how to make friends, Sandy decided. She remembered how she had felt when she first came to this school. Fortunately Carol had been friendly, and soon she felt much better. When Jan turned and walked away, Sandy called, "Jan, wait a minute."

Taking a deep breath, she began, "Carol and I are going ice-skating after school tomorrow. Want to come along? Do you like to skate?"

Jan looked at her instantly. "Do I! I love to skate, but I didn't know where the ice-skating rink was here. And I didn't want to go alone. Sure, I'll ask my mom; I know she'll let me go."

After school the next day she walked along with Sandy and Carol, but said only a few words during the five blocks to the rink. Sandy and Carol talked some, but felt awkward.

Several children from their school entered the rink while the girls were fastening on their skates. The three girls glided down the ice, and Sandy noticed that Jan seemed eager to skate faster. "Let's each skate alone," Sandy suggested. "I want to practice some things I've been trying."

Giving her a smile—almost the first Sandy had seen on her face—Jan slipped away and swirled down the rink. Carol swung around to join Sandy. "Look at her skate!" she said, pointing to Jan. The two watched as Jan skimmed by, straight and tall and graceful. She didn't look like the thin girl standing on the playground with her head forward and her shoulders stooped. In fact, she seemed to have forgotten herself as she spun on the ice and swooped past. As she flashed by she gave the girls another happy smile.

The hour passed quickly. When it was time to go, Jan glided down the length of the rink and spun to a stop right beside Sandy and Carol. "Oh, that was wonderful," she gasped. "I love to ice-skate."

"Where did you learn to skate like that?"

Sandy asked. "I'd like to be able to do those figures."

"It's not hard. But you have to practice a lot."

"Would you help us learn some of those turns and things?" Carol pleaded. "Maybe we could meet here together every week."

"I don't know." Jan spoke slowly, her shoulders slumped.

Sandy turned toward the entrance. "Let's get our skates off and start home. We can talk on the way."

"How long have you been skating?" Carol asked as the three girls headed up the street.

"And where did you learn?" Sandy added. "You must have practiced a lot."

As they walked toward home, Jan told her story. Her father had changed jobs, and the family had had to move away from the town where she had grown up. While he was finding a new place to live, Jan had gone to stay with her grandmother. A rink was nearby, and her grandmother had let her go skating nearly every day. She loved it and liked the school in that town.

"A bunch of us girls skated and did our routines together," Jan said. "We were a team, and it was fun."

"Then your folks moved here, and you had to come with them," Sandy suggested.

"And I didn't want to. I've got two brothers who are always teasing me. They're mean. At

Grandmother's there were just the two of us."

Sandy laughed. "I've got a grandmother too. And when I go there she really spoils me."

"She didn't spoil me." Jan sounded angry. "I'm old enough to do as I please, and she lets me. She wasn't always asking me where I was going and what I was doing. I like doing as I please."

"Do you think we could go skating a couple of times a week and you could teach us some of the things you do?" Sandy persisted. "Maybe we could learn, and then we could have a skating team."

Jan didn't answer for a moment. Finally she said, "I don't think so. My dad says skating costs too much money."

"Yeah, it does." The girls walked on in silence. Then suddenly Sandy exclaimed, "I know! There are two old ladies that live just down the street from us, and they told my mother that they would pay for somebody to help them. We could do that and earn some money. Maybe take turns."

Jan frowned a little. "What do they want done?"

"Oh, stuff like run errands for them, sweep the walk and porches. They're nearly blind, and they can't see to do things like trim the roses. We could do all those things."

"And there is a lady that lives across the street from us that has a baby 2 years old,"

Carol added breathlessly. "She wants some-body just to play with him in the yard so she can get her work done. We could do that."

The three girls went on planning ways of earning money, and Sandy saw that Jan now walked with her head up and a more happy expression.

The next morning at school one of the children who had been at the rink announced when Jan came in, "Oh, Mrs. Moore. You should see Jan skate. She skates better than any of us."

Sandy turned and smiled at Jan, and the girl smiled back. She blushed a rose pink, but sat straight at her desk, not slumping. Mom's idea was a good one, Sandy thought to herself. Jan likes herself better now, and maybe she will like us better too.

Sam's Problem

Sandy knew that Jim was upset about something as soon as they sat down to dinner. He kept picking at his food in silence. Finally, as Sandy served the apple pie, he blurted out, "I'm mad at our teacher's aide. She's getting one of the boys in my room into trouble."

"What do you mean?" his father asked.

"At school today some of the boys were talking about Sam's older brother, Dwight. He goes to high school, you know. The kids say Dwight is selling drugs and is getting Sam to bring the stuff to our school so the kids can try it."

Pausing, Jim pushed his pie to one side. "She heard the boys talking and told the principal. He kept them after school. Why didn't she mind her own business?"

"Oh, Jim," Mother broke in, "it *is* her business. You should be glad someone cares enough about Sam and his brother to get help for them."

"Get help!" Jim burst out. "Do you call it help when she gets Sam into trouble? Sam may have to go to jail."

Father laid down his fork. "I can see you're upset because someone you know may be in trouble. And I understand how you feel. But there is something your friend Sam should know." He paused a moment. "The leaders in a drug ring are always looking for teenagers and even young children to sell drugs for them. Just this week one of the lawyers in our law firm had to go to court to try to get help for a seventh-grade boy who is mixed up in selling drugs."

"A seventh-grade boy?" Sandy broke in. "What happened?"

"A man offered the boy a ten-dollar bill if he would deliver a package of drugs, and the boy did it. One step led to another, until he started to use drugs himself. Then he got another kid to take them too. Finally the police picked him up. That's when the boy's father came to my law partner for advice."

"What do you think will happen to the boy?" Mother asked.

"Since it is his first offense, the court will most likely turn him over to his parents, and they must try to get help for him. You know, Jim, kids your age, and, Sandy, even as young as you, should realize that drug dealers are always looking for people, especially teen-agers, to deliver and even to sell drugs for them. That's why kids like Sam get into real trouble."

Jim nodded in agreement. "But now that Sam is in trouble, what can I do to help him?"

"First of all," Father spoke firmly, "if he offers you drugs, don't touch them. Remember Daniel and his three friends? They wouldn't even eat the fine foods on the king's table so as not to harm their minds.

"Next, don't blame Sam. We don't know what has happened in his home. Maybe there is something my law partner can do to help him. I'll talk to him at the office tomorrow."

"Oh, no!" Jim objected. "If Sam and the other kids found out that you know about this, I'll be in real trouble at school."

"I'll respect your confidence, Jim. But don't be afraid to tell the truth and to stand up for what you know is right."

"Why would they send kids to jail for selling drugs? What's so wrong about drugs? Sam says lots of kids smoke marijauna and it doesn't hurt them."

"Dad"—Sandy turned to her father— "what do drugs do? Why are they bad?"

Her father was serious as he answered her

question. "Some drugs slow down the mind until a person can't think correctly. Others speed up the brain until it burns itself out. Certain drugs damage the brain until a person can never again think as he should. They may ruin the ability to reason."

"That's what Mrs. Hanson said about Old Junky when it was running too fast."

"Old Junky!" Jim demanded. "Who's that?"

Sandy told the story of the old clock that Mr. Knight had put together. "It worked just fine when we put the pendulum back on. Now I understand why Mrs. Hanson said that Old Junky acted like it was on drugs when it was running four times too fast."

Father leaned back in his chair. "That's interesting, Sandy. God created the human brain so that it would think as He does. Our thoughts are important. They make us what we are. The brain records what happens to us—like a computer storing up information. Harmful drugs damage the brain so that people can't think straight or make right decisions. It becomes like a computer that has wires shorted out or circuits damaged. Some drugs destroy the memory, and people don't know who they are while they are under their influence."

"Oh, Dad," Sandy cried. "That would be terrible. I wouldn't even know who I am."

His face grew sad. "That's what happens.

When we harm the brain, we lose the sense of who we are. We forget that God had a plan for our lives, and we are lost."

"And besides that," Mother added, "we get our ideas all mixed up. We even think that harmful things are good for us. Sam said that marijuana doesn't hurt a person, and that's simply not true."

"Why do people use drugs, anyway?" Sandy asked.

Father turned to Jim. "If Sam brought marijuana to school, do you think the kids would try it?"

His son pulled his plate of apple pie back in front of him and took a bite. "Yes, I think some would."

"Why?" Father urged.

"Because some fellows make the kids think it's cool and you're dumb if you don't. Some kids say it's fun, too."

"Yes. Children are naturally curious and want to experiment. But there must be other reasons why people use drugs."

He turned to his wife. "What do you think?"

"Some people think that they can cure everything unpleasant or painful simply by taking a pill. They are used to turning to something they think will make them feel good."

Jim sighed. "I wish someone could get Sam to understand that drugs hurt people."

Sandy looked at her brother. "Why don't you tell him yourself? He likes you a lot, and I think he would listen to you."

"I don't know," Jim mumbled more to himself than anyone else. "I'll have to think about it."

"Let's write down some of the things we've been saying." Mother left the table and returned with a pencil and a sheet of paper. On it she wrote:

What's Wrong With Drugs?
1. Using drugs is an escape from reality.
2. Drugs damage the mind.
3. Drugs may destroy part of the brain.
4. Drugs make it difficult or impossible for a person to understand what God is telling him.

"Mother," Jim said as she finished, "could I have that page?"

She smiled at him and handed him the sheet. "Thanks," he said as he folded it and tucked it into his pocket.

Sandy's Happiness

Sandy ran into the living room before breakfast to pick up a book she had been reading the evening before. Just then her brother came down the stairs from his room.

"Want to see something funny?" He held out a photograph. It was the one he had taken in the hall when Sandy had tripped and fallen with the towels. She saw herself sprawled on the floor with a surprised look on her face. For an instant she felt a flash of anger. Then she thought, If the picture were of someone else, it would be funny. At that moment she could choose to be angry, or she could choose to laugh.

Deciding to laugh, she told her brother, "Come on. Let's show it to Mother and Dad at breakfast."

"You're not mad? Why don't you get angry anymore?"

His sister paused before answering. "I don't have to be angry. I'd rather be happy."

He shrugged. "I guess I could stop teasing, too, if I wanted to."

"Come on." Sandy headed for the dining room. "Let's show the picture to the folks, and may I take it to school? Carol would enjoy seeing it."

As soon as he sat down at the table, Jim displayed the photograph to his parents. After they had all laughed about it, he handed it to Sandy to take to school. Then Jim turned to his father. "Dad, Sam says he would like to talk to you about this drug business. Could you speak to him if he comes here? I think maybe you can help him know what he should do."

"Of course, Jim. I'll be glad to talk with him anytime, and I feel sure I can help him."

"Thanks, Dad. I'll tell him. Maybe he can stop by tonight."

School had not begun when Sandy ran into the classroom, but Carol was already there. She laid the picture of herself on Carol's desk. "Want to see something funny?"

Carol laughed. "Oh, look at the expression on your face!" Both girls were laughing so hard they didn't see their teacher and Mrs. Hanson as they walked down the aisle.

"Can we share in your laugh?" Mrs. Moore asked.

Sandy showed them the picture and told the story of what had happened. After they had enjoyed the incident together, Mrs. Hanson became serious. "Sandy, you've discovered a wonderful secret that is going to make your life happier. You can choose what your actions will be. And with God's help you can make the right choices. I am happy for you."

"I'm happy too." Sandy tucked the picture into her purse. "And I'll try to remember what you have taught us. It has helped me to make the right choices."

When the bell rang, the children quickly took their seats. Mrs. Moore glanced around the classroom. "Boys and girls, today is Mrs. Hanson's last day with us. Some of you may want to talk with her about what you have learned and what has happened to you."

"I'd like to tell about my little sister," Carol began. "For a long time I've been wishing I had my own room with a lock on the door. Then my sister would have to leave my things alone. Finally I decided she was big enough to choose to stay out of my things. I told her about her will and the little judges that would help her choose what was right to do. And guess what she said! She wanted to play with my things because she wanted to be big like me and have big girls' things. She cried about it, too. I just didn't know how she felt. And I've been mean to her . . ." Carol stopped.

"How did you and your sister work out your problem?" Mrs. Hanson probed gently.

Carol's face brightened. "Oh, I went through my drawers and let her pick out five things that she wanted. Then we cleaned out one drawer, and that is hers now. She can play that she is grown-up. And she promised to leave all the rest of my things alone. Besides that, I am spending some time every day just playing with her. We're having fun, and it makes her happy."

"That was a thoughtful way to treat your little sister. Choosing to think What would Jesus do? is very rewarding, isn't it?" Mrs. Hanson looked around the room. "Would someone else like to tell us about making a choice? Did anyone make a poor choice?"

Jeff raised his hand. "I think I did yesterday. I went over to the park to play ball, and my mother said I must be home by six. But I didn't make it."

"Did you forget to look at your watch?"

"No, I looked. But I decided that I wouldn't leave. I'd be up to bat next, and I decided to stay, even if I got punished. So I played and then ran home, but I was pretty late."

"What happened?" Tim asked.

"Did you get punished?" Mike wanted to know.

"No, but when I got home no one was there

but my grandmother. She was sitting in the living room sewing. I asked, Where is everybody?"

"She said, 'They're gone. They couldn't wait any longer.' My dad had come home early, and the whole family had gone to my uncle's place. Then they left for the lake for a picnic and boating." Jeff shook his head. "I wished that I hadn't decided to stay and finish the ball game."

"But you didn't know." Carol's voice was full of sympathy.

"I'm sorry, Jeff, that you missed the good time," Mrs. Hanson said, and the children agreed. They all knew how it felt. "It's hard to learn lessons that way, but they are the ones we remember longest. Does someone else have an experience to tell? What about you, Sandy? Is your brother still teasing you?"

"Sometimes, but I don't let it bother me so much." She wanted to tell the woman more, but was embarrassed to express how she felt before all the children. She wished to let her know that because she was changing, Jim was too. He had even offered to let her use his camera. The night before, he had brought it into the dining room and showed her a little bit about how to operate it.

Jeff glanced across at her. "Don't you still get mad?"

"A little." Shyly Sandy rolled her pencil between her fingers.

"There's a good verse in the Bible for you."
Mrs. Hanson picked up the *Good News Bible* on
the desk and read: "'A gentle answer quiets
anger.' King Solomon wrote that. It's Proverbs 15:1."

"Oh, he isn't angry when he teases me,"
Sandy defended her brother. "He does it just
for fun. And when I don't get angry, everything is OK."

"You are showing real understanding,"
Mrs.Hanson commented with approval. "Just
keep on and you'll win the battle. I don't think
brothers dislike sisters. They just don't know
how to be friends sometimes, and they tease
to get attention."

Several children agreed. Then Jan raised
her hand. "I still think brothers like to be
mean. My brothers try to boss me, and I hate
it. And then I feel mad at everybody." She
twisted her hands together and didn't look at
the other children.

"How do you think you might change the
way you feel?" Mrs. Hanson asked gently.

"I don't know. I think all this about little
judges and talking to yourself about what you
should do is silly." She stopped, embarrassed.

"Are you willing to think about that some
more?" Mrs. Hanson's voice was gentle.

Jan nodded. "I guess so." She raised her
head and looked at Sandy and then at Carol,
and a tiny smile played around her mouth.

"It takes real courage on your part, Jan, to face your feelings." Mrs. Hanson sympathized. "And no matter how you feel, Jesus loves you just the way you are. But He loves you too much to leave you just that way. He is willing to help you make the right choices."

Sandy saw Mike twisting in his seat as though he wanted to speak. Then she saw him raise his hand. As soon as Mrs. Hanson turned to him, he blurted, "I'd like to say something."

"Fine. Tell us your story."

"I didn't believe you when you said that God would help us say the right thing, and that we could choose for Him to help us. But I found out you were right."

"Tell us what happened."

"Well, I guess I'm just like my dad," Mike continued. "He explodes sometimes, and he doesn't even think about what he's saying. Other times I can talk to him about anything and he doesn't get mad.

"Dad and I went camping over the weekend. We backpacked into the mountains and found a nice place to camp. And we had a real good time. While we were sitting by the campfire, Dad asked me how things were going at school. He wanted to know what I was learning. Before I knew it I told him everything that's been bothering me, and about my getting mad. Then I explained to him what we've been discovering about how our brains work. I even told him about conscience, and reason, and desire, and how we are happier when they all want the same thing."

"You remember well, Mike. And what did your father say about that?"

He didn't say anything for a while, and I was afraid I'd made him mad. Then he said that I was right. And maybe from now on he should ask God to help him."

The children listened quietly, for they knew how much it would mean to Mike to have his father learn to follow God.

"Thank you, Mike," Mrs. Hanson said, "for sharing this personal experience with us. Let's all thank God for the way He leads and cares for us." As the children bowed their heads, she prayed, "Thank You, God, that You do not use force of any kind to make us obey You. Thank You for helping us to make right decisions. Amen."

Then she gave each of the children a sheet of paper with the motto they had been learning printed on it. A border of flowers surrounded the words. Sandy thought the motto would look nice framed.

"Plant a thought, reap a feeling," Sandy read to herself. The words had puzzled her, but now she understood what they meant. She looked through the window at the flowering trees. The tulips in the window box had faded, and Mrs. Moore had replaced them with yellow flowers that glowed like gold in the morning sunshine. The bright spring day reflected the happiness Sandy felt. In just a few days summer vacation would begin. With God's help she would choose to make every day a happy one for the whole family.